# i've been Pi_____

## CHOPPER'S "TAIL" OF ADOPTION

For Andre, Mario, Shadow and ALL adopted children and pets ~~EXCEPT~~ cats. including

*Mommy made me change it!*

## by CHOPPER STEEDLEY-TOLAN
### (with a little help from Mommy)

*AuthorHouse™*
*1663 Liberty Drive*
*Bloomington, IN 47403*
*www.authorhouse.com*
*Phone: 1-800-839-8640*

Lots of Licks!

Chopper

*First published by AuthorHouse    7/12/2011*

*ISBN: 978-1-4634-3554-7 (sc)*

*Library of Congress Control Number: 2011911541*

*Printed in the United States of America*

*Any people depicted in stock imagery provided by Thinkstock are models,*
*and such images are being used for illustrative purposes only.*
*Certain stock imagery © Thinkstock.*

*This book is printed on acid-free paper.*

authorHOUSE®

Hi! My name is Chopper and I'm a dog.

I'm adopted, black and white, hairy and short, and my belly is full of freckles. I was adopted from my birth parents by Mommy and Daddy when I was only two months old. Back then my name was George.

Mommy and Daddy saw our ad and came to visit. Ringo and I were the only puppies left. I REALLY wanted to go home with them, but I was smaller so I thought they would pick my brother instead of me. Boy, was I WRONG! Mommy fell in love with me when she saw my picture and KNEW I would be her puppy!

SHIH TZU PUPPIES

$ priceless

That's me on top of my brothers, John, Paul and Ringo.

| Pet Type | Age |
| --- | --- |
| Dog | --- |
| Pet Breed | Color |
| Shih Tzu | --- |
| Neutered | Pet Sex |
| No | --- |
| Pet License | |
| 137246 | |

Description
4 Male Shih Tzu Puppies, 2 Brown, Black & White, 2 Black & White, Family Raised With Both Parents, Mother Is AKC Registered, Father Is CKC Registered, Absolutely Adorable! Born On 12/10/08, 6 1/2 weeks Old And Ready To Go! Picture Taken On 1/23/09

Mommy and Daddy were SO happy I was their puppy, they didn't even mind when I got excited and scared and sick at my tummy in the car on the way home.

They just showed me my new room, gave me dinner,

a new bone to chew,

and a new toy to play with.

As soon as I got used to my forever Mommy and Daddy, I met my brother Kyle.

Ther

Mario

He's a boy, and hairy like me, but he's not adopted.

met Uncle Bob, Aunt Terri and my cousins, Mario, Andre and Shadow.

My cousins are ALL boys and ALL adopted just like me!

They aren't adopted, but they gave me peanut butter AND let me play in the curtains.

Next, I flew across the country to meet Grandma and Grandpa.

After meeting some of my new family,
I figured out that sometimes you look
JUST like your forever family ...

... and sometimes you don't really look like them at all.

Even if you don't LOOK alike, if you REALLY look close you can find lots of ways you ARE alike.

Uncle Bob

Aunt Ter

🐾 Mario, Shadow, Bob and I all like to run.

🐾 Bob and Mario like to pla golf, have green eyes an a slender build.

🐾 Andre and Bob LOVE to eat ice cream.

🐾 Andre and Terri both like to dance.

🐾 Mario and Terri like to play board games.

🐾 Terri, Andre, Shadow and I like to play tennis, have brown eyes and an athletic build.

Andre

Shadow

Mario

🐾 All six of us have at least some dark hair, like to eat pizza, swim and ride bicycles or motorcycles.

Four-Legged Friends!

After I saw how much I have in common with my adopted family members, I was ready to meet ALL kinds of friends in my neighborhood ...

Adopted Friends

His name Choppe too!

Young Friends

Two-Wheeled Friends

American Indian Friends

Silly Friends

Four-Wheeled Friends

Happy Friends

**and all over the country!**

Flying Aunts

Little Cousins

Road Trip Aunts

East Coast Friends

Little Friends

A Friend Named Zig

Big Friends

Before long my life was filled with all different shapes,

Furry Friends

California Cousins

sizes and kinds of friends and family members.

Fancy Friends

Freaky Friends

Since my forever Mommy and Daddy
want me to grow up to be a
responsible, obedient dog,
they make sure I go to school,

and take me to the park to learn to play well with other dogs.

They also teach me to share my
    toys with my friends (and Daddy)
and to help with the chores.

She's Zig's Mommy too!

Soon I needed a check-up. That's when I met Dr. Raymond. Since I'm a dog, she's called a vet. She gives me shots, and sometimes medicine, to make sure I stay healthy. I also met my doggy dentist, Miss Joanne. She cleans my teeth to keep them shiny, clean and strong.

that's me in the blanket!

When it was time for a bath and my first haircut, I went to see Miss Pat and Miss Carla.

That's Miss Pat! ⬅

I was VERY hairy before my first haircut, but Miss Pat and Miss Carla were so nice it wasn't scary at all! ⬆

It REALLY tickles when she cuts my hair, but being all soft when she's finished is worth being tickled. ⬅

# After a year filled with lots more firsts, like...

hot air ballooning in Alabama,

cheering Mommy's favorite team to a National Championship,

sailing my fish boat in the swimming pool and

riding on Mommy's motorcycle...

...I celebrated my first birthday with my forever Mommy and Daddy and friends I have made since I was adopted.

Mommy even made me a dog food, cheese, green bean and peanut butter birthday cake. YUMMY!

Then I celebrated my very first Christmas with my forever family at Grandma and Grandpa's house.

I like hanging out under our living room tree and looking at all the shiny lights and presents.

I had SO much fun I fell asleep with some of my toys in my bed!

I wore my Santa suit AND I found a big sock with my name on it filled with toys and treats!

Now that I've been adopted for a whole year, sometimes I remember when I first came home with Mommy and Daddy. I tried really hard to be a good boy, but it didn't always work.

I chewed my way out when I was supposed to stay in.

I hid from Mommy under the bookcase.

I used Daddy's jacket as a chew toy.

Since I'm a big boy now, I seem to find more ways to have fun that get me in bigger trouble, like ...

exploring my cousins' HUGE dog house when my uncle told me not to,

enjoying the only mud buddle at the park,

and boinging ribbons on presents under the living room tree.

But no matter how much trouble I get into, or how little or big I am, Mommy and Daddy still love me because I'm their dog.

Sometimes I dream about my birth parents and wonder where they are or what it would be like to live with them.

I even get sad when I think about them, but I'm always glad when I remember that my forever Mommy and Daddy PICKED ME. Being adopted is pretty cool!

# Extra Big Thank Yous To:

Mario, Andre, Shadow, Aunt Terri and Uncle Bob

My Family, Friends and Neighbors who let
Mommy take their pictures for my book

Dr. Raymond, Miss Joanne, Miss Pat and Miss Carla

Miss LeeAnn, Miss Tricia, and Lucy & Oliver's Mommy

And of course, Daddy and all of my other friends who
inspired me and helped me with my very first book

CPSIA information can be obtained
at www.ICGtesting.com
Printed in the USA
238548LV00001B